To Angela, Antonello, Daniele, Elena and Laura,
the points where my journey begins.

The Journey © Flying Eye Books 2016.

This is a first edition published in 2016 by Flying Eye Books,
an imprint of Nobrow Ltd. 62 Great Eastern Street, London, EC2A 3QR.

All characters, illustrations and text © Francesca Sanna 2016. Francesca Sanna has asserted her right under
the Copyright, Designs and Patents Act, 1988, to be identified as the Author and Illustrator of this Work.

Published in the US by Nobrow (US) Inc.
Printed in Latvia on FSC assured paper.

ISBN: 978-1-909263-99-4

Order from www.flyingeyebooks.com

The Journey

by Francesca Sanna

Flying Eye Books

London–New York

I live with my family in a city close to the sea. Every summer we used to spend many weekends at the beach. But we never go there anymore, because last year, our lives changed forever...

The war began. Every day bad things
started happening around us and
soon there was nothing but chaos.

And one day the war took my father.

Since that day everything has become darker
and my mother has become more and more worried.

The other day, one of my mother's friends told her that
many people are leaving. They are trying to escape to another
country. A country far away with high mountains.

"What is this place?" we ask our mother.

"It is a safe place," she tells us.

"And where is this place?" we ask again.

She shows us pictures of strange cities, strange forests and strange animals
until she finally sighs, "We will go there and not be frightened anymore."

We don't want to leave but our mother tells us it
will be a great adventure. We put everything we have
in suitcases and say goodbye to everyone we know.

We leave at night to avoid being seen...

and keep moving for many days.

The further we go...

We finally arrive at the border.

It is an enormous wall
and we must climb over it!

But, oh NO!

"You are not allowed to
cross the border. Go back!"
shouts an angry guard.

We have nowhere to go
and we are very tired.

In the darkness the noises
of the forest scare me.

But mother is with us
and she is never scared.
We close our eyes and
finally fall asleep.

Shouting wakes us up. It's the guards!
They are looking for us and we must hide.

"Quick! This way,"
whispers our mother.

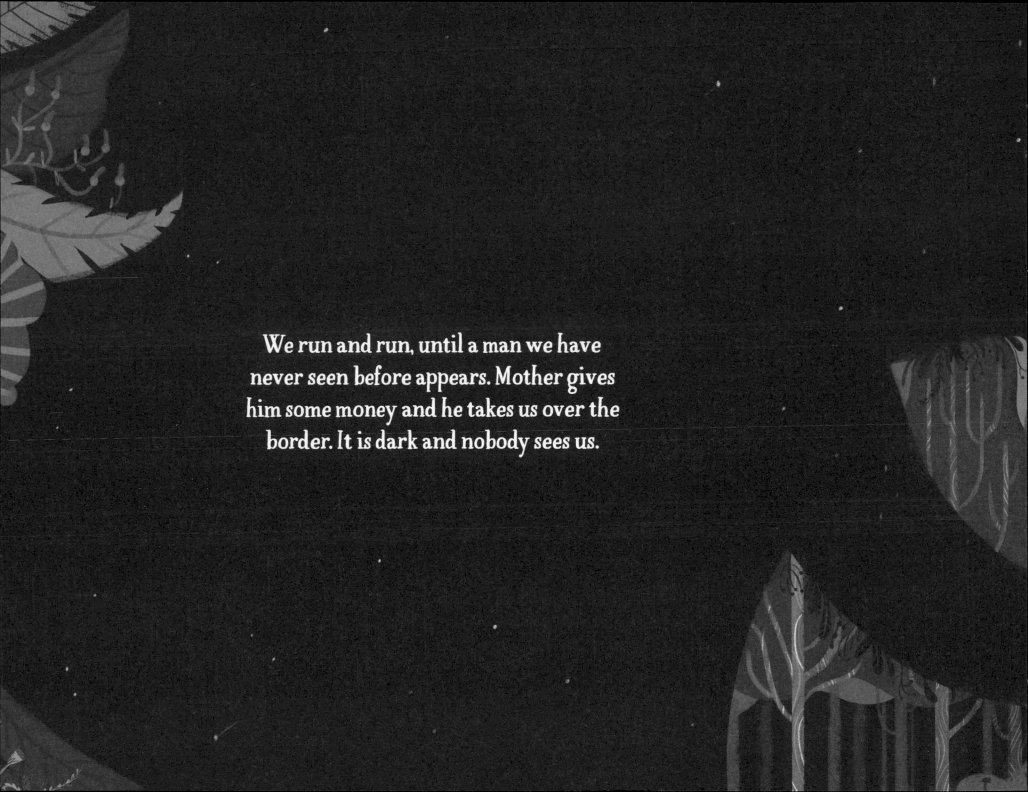

We run and run, until a man we have
never seen before appears. Mother gives
him some money and he takes us over the
border. It is dark and nobody sees us.

"Our journey is not over yet," our mother tells us. The sea stretches
far and wide ahead of us and we must cross it. How will this be possible?

We have boarded a ferry with so many people!
There is not much space and it rains every day,
but we tell each other stories. Tales of terrible and
dangerous monsters that hide beneath our boat,
ready to gobble us up if the boat capsizes!

The boat rocks and rocks as the waves
grow bigger and bigger. It feels like the sea will
never end. We tell each other new stories. Stories
about the land we are heading to, where the big
green forests are filled with kind fairies that dance
and give us magic spells to end the war.

As the sun rises, we see land for the first time in days. The boat rocks
silently to shore. Our mother tells us we are very lucky to still be together.
"Is this the place where we will be safe?" we ask.
"It is close," she says with a tired smile.

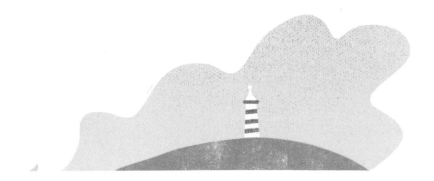

We travel for more days and more nights, crossing many borders.

From the train I look up to the birds that seem to be following us...

They are migrating just like us. And their journey
is very long too, but they don't have to cross any borders.

I hope, one day, like these birds, we will find a new home.
A home where we can be safe and begin our story again.

Author's note

"The Journey" is actually a story about many journeys, and it began with the story of two girls I met in a refugee centre in Italy. After meeting them I realized that behind their journey lay something very powerful. So I began collecting more stories of migration and interviewing many people from many different countries. A few months later, in September 2014, when I started studying a Master of Arts in illustration at the Academy of Lucerne, I knew I wanted to create a book about these true stories. Almost every day on the news we hear the terms 'migrants' and 'refugees' but we rarely ever speak to or hear the personal journeys that they have had to take. This book is a collage of all those personal stories and the incredible strength of the people within them.